HIP-HOP

- Alicia Keys
- Ashanti
- Beyoncé
- Black Eyed Peas
- Busta Rhymes
- Chris Brown
- Christina Aguilera
- Ciara
- Cypress Hill
- Daddy Yankee
- DMX
- Don Omar
- Dr. Dre
- Eminem
- Fat Joe
- 50 Cent
- The Game
- Hip-Hop: A Short History
- Hip-Hop Around the World
- Ice Cube
- Ivy Queen
- Jay-Z
- Jennifer Lopez
- Juelz Santana
- Kanye West
- Lil Wayne
- LL Cool J
- Lloyd Banks
- Ludacris
- Mariah Carey
- Mary J. Blige
- Missy Elliot
- Nas
- Nelly
- Notorious B.I.G.
- OutKast
- Pharrell Williams
- Pitbull
- Queen Latifah
- Reverend Run (of Run DMC)
- Sean "Diddy" Combs
- Snoop Dogg
- T.I.
- Tupac
- Usher
- Will Smith
- Wu-Tang Clan
- Xzibit
- Young Jeezy
- Yung Joc

His name says it all: Busta Rhymes is one of the best rhymers in the world of hip-hop. And in a genre that depends on rhyme, that's saying a lot!

Hip-Hop

Busta Rhymes

Toby G. Hamilton

Mason Crest Publishers

Busta Rhymes

Copyright © 2008 by Mason Crest Publishers. All rights reserved. No part of this publication may be reproduced or transmitted in any form or by any means, electronic or mechanical, including photocopying, recording, taping, or any information storage and retrieval system, without permission from the publisher.

Produced by Harding House Publishing Service, Inc.
201 Harding Avenue, Vestal, NY 13850.

MASON CREST PUBLISHERS INC.
370 Reed Road
Broomall, Pennsylvania 19008
(866)MCP-BOOK (toll free)
www.masoncrest.com

Printed in the United States of America

First Printing

9 8 7 6 5 4 3 2 1

Library of Congress Cataloging-in-Publication Data

Hamilton, Toby G.
  Busta Rhymes / Toby G. Hamilton.
      p. cm. — (Hip-hop)
  Includes bibliographical references and index.
  ISBN: 978-1-4222-0284-5
  ISBN: 978-1-4222-0077-3 (series)

  1. Busta Rhymes (Musician)—Juvenile literature. 2. Rap musicians—United States—Biography—Juvenile literature. 3. Actors—United States—Biography—Juvenile literature. I. Title.
  ML3930.B93H36 2008
  782.421649092--dc22
  [B]
                                2007031166

Publisher's notes:
- All quotations in this book come from original sources and contain the spelling and grammatical inconsistencies of the original text.

- The Web sites mentioned in this book were active at the time of publication. The publisher is not responsible for Web sites that have changed their addresses or discontinued operation since the date of publication. The publisher will review and update the Web site addresses each time the book is reprinted.

DISCLAIMER: The following story has been thoroughly researched, and to the best of our knowledge, represents a true story. While every possible effort has been made to ensure accuracy, the publisher will not assume liability for damages caused by inaccuracies in the data, and makes no warranty on the accuracy of the information contained herein. This story has not been authorized nor endorsed by Busta Rhymes.

Contents

Hip-Hop Time Line	6
1 Busta: A King of the Hip-Hop World	9
2 Born at the Right Time	21
3 Hitting the Charts and the Silver Screen	31
4 The New Millennium	39
5 Number One for the First Time	47
Chronology	54
Accomplishments and Awards	56
Further Reading/Internet Resources	59
Glossary	61
Index	63
About the Author	64
Picture Credits	64

Hip-Hop Time Line

1970s DJ Kool Herc pioneers the use of breaks, isolations, and repeats using two turntables.

1970s Grafitti artist Vic begins tagging on New York subways.

1976 Grandmaster Flash and the Furious Five emerge as one of the first battlers and freestylers.

1982 Afrika Bambaataa tours Europe in another hip-hop first.

1980 Rapper Kurtis Blow sells a million records and makes the first nationwide TV appearance for a hip-hop artist.

1984 The track "Roxanne Roxanne" sparks the first diss war.

1988 Hip-hop record sales reach 100 million annually.

1985 The film *Krush Groove*, about the rise of Def Jam Records, is released.

1970   1980

1970s The central elements of the hip-hop culture begin to emerge in the Bronx, New York City.

1974 Afrika Bambaataa organizes the Universal Zulu Nation.

1979 "Rapper's Delight," by The Sugarhill Gang, goes gold.

1981 Grandmaster Flash and the Furious Five release *Adventures on the Wheels of Steel*.

1983 Ice-T releases his first singles, marking the earliest examples of gangsta rap.

1984 *Grafitti Rock*, the first hip-hop television program, premieres.

1986 Run DMC cover Aerosmith's "Walk this Way" and appear on the cover of *Rolling Stone*.

1988 MTV premieres *Yo! MTV Raps*.

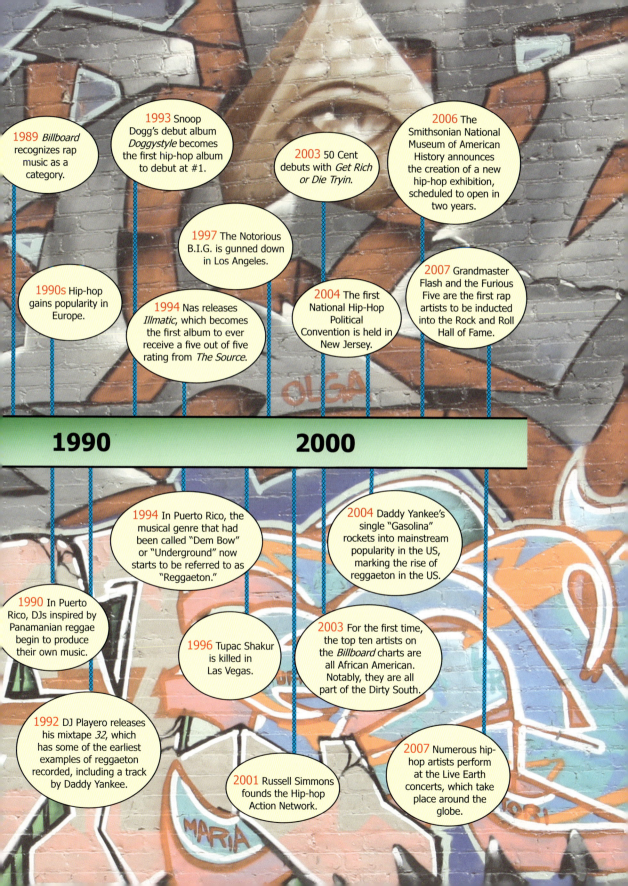

1989 *Billboard* recognizes rap music as a category.

1993 Snoop Dogg's debut album *Doggystyle* becomes the first hip-hop album to debut at #1.

2003 50 Cent debuts with *Get Rich or Die Tryin*.

2006 The Smithsonian National Museum of American History announces the creation of a new hip-hop exhibition, scheduled to open in two years.

1997 The Notorious B.I.G. is gunned down in Los Angeles.

1990s Hip-hop gains popularity in Europe.

1994 Nas releases *Illmatic*, which becomes the first album to ever receive a five out of five rating from *The Source*.

2004 The first National Hip-Hop Political Convention is held in New Jersey.

2007 Grandmaster Flash and the Furious Five are the first rap artists to be inducted into the Rock and Roll Hall of Fame.

1990   2000

1994 In Puerto Rico, the musical genre that had been called "Dem Bow" or "Underground" now starts to be referred to as "Reggaeton."

2004 Daddy Yankee's single "Gasolina" rockets into mainstream popularity in the US, marking the rise of reggaeton in the US.

1990 In Puerto Rico, DJs inspired by Panamanian reggae begin to produce their own music.

1996 Tupac Shakur is killed in Las Vegas.

2003 For the first time, the top ten artists on the *Billboard* charts are all African American. Notably, they are all part of the Dirty South.

1992 DJ Playero releases his mixtape *32*, which has some of the earliest examples of reggaeton recorded, including a track by Daddy Yankee.

2001 Russell Simmons founds the Hip-hop Action Network.

2007 Numerous hip-hop artists perform at the Live Earth concerts, which take place around the globe.

In a career that spans more than a decade and a half, Busta Rhymes has become a legend on the hip-hop scene. But his influence goes beyond music. In 2004, Busta appeared at the MTV VMA Vote or Die Pre-Party.

1

Busta: A King of the Hip-Hop World

Busta Rhymes is a legend. In the hip-hop music industry, the average artist's career lasts only three years. In that time, they could put out three albums. They might even have some #1 hits. The glory comes fast . . . but it leaves even faster. Most hip-hop artists that blow up big quickly fizzle out. Not Busta Rhymes. He's now been in the business more than fifteen years. He's had seven solo studio albums with an eighth on its way. He's also put out greatest hits albums, **compilation** albums, and records with many other artists. And even after all this time, fans agree that Busta Rhymes keeps getting better.

The Man, the Musician

Today, Busta Rhymes is a famous musician, an actor, and a superstar. But in an interview with Melanie J. Cornish for nobodysmiling.com, Busta Rhymes insisted that he is just a regular guy:

> "I am just a regular person and I love to work and I love to make music. I am a Father, I am a son and I am a brother and I strive to do what I do with this music and I put most of my time . . . into that. But outside of that I am a dude that just does the regular [stuff] that people do, movies, like to drive my car, like to go shopping, spend time with my family."

Busta might just be a regular guy when he's sitting at home with his family, but out on the street, he is anything but average. He can't go anywhere without bodyguards. He lives in the spotlight. He gives interviews and appears on television shows. People want to know his opinion on everything from the state of the music industry to politics. He has legions of fans, and wherever he goes, he is asked for his autograph. And it's all because of his music.

Busta Rhymes's music is called hardcore rap. It's a type of hip-hop music that features heavy beats, ripping **samples**, and tough, aggressive lyrics. Hardcore hip-hop is **controversial** because it contains lots of profanity and violent themes. In fact, the most hardcore rap (specifically gangsta rap) is often criticized for promoting and glorifying guns, drugs, violence, and gang life. But hardcore hip-hop is also famous for its social and political content. Hardcore rap songs often talk about weighty issues like poverty, racism, crime, and other harsh realities of inner-city streets. Hardcore rap, and hip-hop music in general, has played a significant role in bringing a lot of these inner-city issues out into the open. Busta Rhymes's

Rap music has a controversial reputation. Many critics condemn the music, especially gangsta and Busta's hardcore, for the way it sometimes glorifies violence. Others say the musicians are just revealing what's real.

music isn't gangsta rap, but it is hardcore. Throughout his career he has been criticized for his profanity and explicit lyrics, but he's also received much praise for his party-hearty songs that keep the mood light and the clubs hopping.

In addition to being hardcore, Busta Rhymes is also an East Coast hip-hop artist. Hip-hop music is very regional, with different forms of the music coming from different areas of the country. Today there's East Coast, West Coast, Dirty South, and other hip-hop styles. East Coast hip-hop could be called

In the 1970s, many inner cities found themselves in a state of decay. To remedy some of the problems faced by the inner cities, high-rise apartment buildings were constructed to house low-income people. Though the goal might have been admirable, for the most part the results weren't.

BUSTA: A KING OF THE HIP-HOP WORLD

the original form of hip-hop music, since hip-hop music got its start on the East Coast in New York City in the 1970s. Busta was a child in New York when early DJs laid down those first hip-hop tracks and made music history. Little did he know that one day he would become an important part of that history and a king of the hip-hop world.

From the Street Up

The hip-hop music movement all began in the Bronx, a region of New York City. It was the 1970s, and times were hard. The Bronx in that era was made up mostly of black and Latino neighborhoods. Many people struggled with poverty. People living in "the projects"—apartment buildings and neighborhoods designed for people with low incomes—faced high crime rates. Many of the inner-city schools were poor and deteriorating, and there were few opportunities for young people to advance to a better position in life. Racism was also a major problem, and it affected every aspect of life in the ghetto.

The Bronx also had large immigrant communities. The United States has always been a country of immigrants, and as newcomers arrive on American shores, they bring their arts, *culture*, and experiences with them. In the United States, art and culture from all over the world come together, influence each other, and inspire new forms of expression. Overall, many living in Bronx neighborhoods (and in many urban areas around the country) were seething with frustration, dissatisfaction, and an urge to rebel. Music was one way that they would express these feelings and rebel against their circumstances. In the Bronx in the 1970s, a Jamaican immigrant who called himself Kool Herc introduced part of his culture to the Bronx music scene. His contribution changed American music forever and gave birth to hip-hop.

This birth happened at the club, house, and block parties that were so popular in the Bronx and other areas of the city.

Kool Herc was one of many mobile DJs in New York City at the time. In the seventies, disco, **funk**, jazz, and soul were some of the most popular forms of music, and dancing was a favorite pastime. In the troubled Bronx neighborhoods, people didn't have a lot of money for expensive forms of entertainment, but mobile DJs could bring great music to them. Parties with music and dancing were an affordable way to have a great time, and a mobile DJ could get a party started virtually anywhere, anytime. In fact, they even got parties going on the streets and in the parks, making music and dancing a very public affair.

Hip-hop was born at these parties when DJ Kool Herc introduced some Jamaican presentation styles to his shows. He would set up two turntables, each with a copy of the same record. Then he'd isolate the "break" of the song, the part that contains just the beat. The break is the best part of a song for dancing, but it is also usually very short. To keep the dancing going, Kool Herc would get both turntables spinning. Then, when the break ended on the one record, he'd switch to the break on the other record. When that break ended, he'd switch back again. With the aid of a mixer, he could go back and forth between the two records, blending the breaks together to keep the beat going as long as he liked. By doing this, he allowed partygoers to dance on and on, and the partiers loved him for it.

Almost immediately, other DJs began copying and adapting Kool Herc's style. Soon they weren't just mixing back and forth between two copies of the same record. They began mixing different records, taking breaks and samples from multiple songs and putting them together to create a whole new piece of music. They also jumped on another Jamaican element that Kool Herc used in his shows, something called "toasting." During a show, a DJ would toast or "shout out" to the crowd over the microphone. The toasts started out simply, with introductions, jokes, and boasts. But soon they got more complex. Parties began having MCs—people who just worked the mic—who kept the show entertaining and lively while the music played. The MCs took toasting to a whole new level by speaking in rhythm and rhyme to the music. They called the style rapping, and before long the MCs were stealing the show. The two fundamental elements of hip-hop music—cutting and mixing the beats and rapping—were now complete.

So what do you do when you're young and poor and live in the inner city? You listen to music. DJs and MCs brought entertainment to the streets. Music was also a way that some lucky and talented individuals were able to escape poverty.

A Cultural Revolution

As hip-hop music spread and gained popularity, a cultural revolution began on the streets. People, especially young men, started rapping, not just at parties, but when hanging out at school, in the parks, and on the street corners. Rapping was a way a guy could show his skills and get respect from his peers. MCs confronted each other in toe-to-toe, freestyle battles of rhythm, rhyme, and wit. If there was no DJ or boom box for the music, a beat boxer could provide the beat with his mouth, hands, throat, and voice. The best MCs earned local reputations and had posses of followers.

With the birth of the Zulu Nation, hip-hop got even bigger. A New York DJ named Afrika Bambaataa started the Nation. Bambaataa (like many people who became hip-hop artists) had been a gang member, but after visiting Africa and learning about the history of the Zulu people, he decided to turn his life around. He came back to his home in the South Bronx wanting to contribute and help make the black community stronger, rather than weakening it through gang violence and crime. He saw hip-hop music as a way to get out his message. He realized that hip-hop music could help people raise themselves up, be part of something positive, and help educate others. He began The Organization, which would later be called the Zulu Nation, and then the Universal Zulu Nation. The Organization hosted cultural events with dancing and music for young people. It encouraged kids to turn away from the dangers of the streets, and it greatly contributed to the spread of hip-hop music.

Other people, including break-dancers, graffiti artists, and reformed gang members, began joining the Zulu Nation. It quickly became clear that hip-hop wasn't just about music. It was a whole cultural movement, involving all different ways of expressing life on the streets of inner-city America. It was the music of the streets, the dancing of the streets, the art, the fashion, and the language of the streets. New forms of street dance, like break dancing, popping, and locking, became integral parts of hip-hop culture. While hip-hop music boomed from a stereo, b-boys (break-dancers) would get down with complex footwork, flips, spins, handstands, and crazy moves.

Tagging, or graffiti, also became a big part of hip-hop culture. Taggers put their names on public spaces, like subway cars and bridges, to announce their presence, gain fame, and claim a space as theirs. But as hip-hop culture grew, tagging became more self-conscious, purposeful, and ambitious. The tags became stylized, colorful, and complex. As graffiti developed into an art form, it became as much a part of urban street culture as hip-hop music and dancing.

Spreading the Word

Hip-hop culture, with its music, art, and dancing, was a way for young people from the inner city, a place where poverty, crime, fear, and hopelessness reigned, to express themselves and earn recognition and respect. It had all just started with party music and people trying to have a good time. But with the birth of the Zulu Nation and other politically minded artists, hip-hop culture developed goals and a message. The goal: to improve life on the streets. The message: America has denied the inner-city's existence for too long; it's time to rise up, speak for ourselves, and take control of our destiny.

Hip-hop culture, with its daring, pride, and bravado, quickly moved from the Bronx to other parts of New York City. Before long, hip-hop was spreading to other metropolitan areas. Baltimore, Philadelphia, Miami, Detroit, Houston, Los Angeles—all around America, inner-city kids were being inspired by this new music and starting to create it themselves. By the late 1980s, that music was hitting the *mainstream*, and larger American population heard rap for the first time. As its popularity grew, it went overseas and eventually became one of the most popular forms of music in the world. Today, music,

Some hip-hop dancers seemed to have superhuman moves—or at least moves that make their bodies seem to be made of elastic. Break dancing began in the clubs, but before long, break-dancers could be found performing on many New York City street corners.

art, fashion, and language have all been affected by hip-hop culture.

As the first hip-hop acts formed on the streets, a young boy named Trevor Smith was listening. In those early years, no one thought about becoming famous doing hip-hop. The MCs, DJs, b-boys, and graffiti artists were just expressing themselves. But some DJs and MCs started cutting records. Then some visionary music executives began offering a few hip-hop artists record deals. Most people thought hip-hop music was just a fad that would end as quickly as it began, but a few people knew it could be more. By the time Trevor was a teenager, hip-hop was all over urban radio and beginning to break through to the mainstream. For the first time, people began realizing that they could do more than just rap in clubs and on the streets. They could actually have music careers. Trevor started rapping and began to think that he just might have a future in the spotlight.

Trevor Tahiem Smith Jr., the future Busta Rhymes, grew up in Brooklyn, a borough of New York City. Not far away, in another of the city's boroughs, hip-hop was also growing up. Little did the city know how important the boy and the music would be to each other.

Born at the Right Time

Trevor Tahiem Smith Jr. was born on May 20, 1972, in Brooklyn, a borough of New York City. His parents were Jamaican immigrants, and his neighborhood had many families of West Indian (Caribbean) origin. Like most of the kids in his neighborhood, Trevor loved sports. Cable and satellite TV weren't as common as they are today, and there were none of the computers and gaming systems that now keep young people indoors, so kids had to make their own fun. In Trevor's Brooklyn neighborhood, they did that mostly with games they played in the street. Trevor and his friends often played soccer. They'd also knock the bottom out of a milk crate, nail it up on a light pole, and shoot hoops.

The Early Years

Trevor's family was quite traditional. In interviews, he has described his mother as a very tough disciplinarian. His father was a self-employed electrical engineer. His parents were passionate people with strong convictions, and their attitudes shaped Trevor as he grew. He learned self-respect and a strong work ethic from his parents. They taught young Trevor that, to have success in this world, he'd need to know who he was, and he'd have to stand up for himself and his beliefs. He would begin doing that in his music early on, and today he says his parents are largely responsible for who he is as a person and as an artist.

Like the Bronx, many Brooklyn neighborhoods had problems with poverty, crime, and drugs. By the early 1980s, a crack epidemic was raging in New York City. For decades, people had been moving to the suburbs to escape the problems of the inner city. When Trevor was twelve, his parents decided it was time for their family to make that move as well. They left their Brooklyn neighborhood for a suburb of Long Island called Uniondale.

At Uniondale, Trevor's love of sports continued, and he became one of the best basketball players at the school. His classroom work, however, didn't hold his interest, and he wasn't all that committed to his high school education. And as much as he loved basketball and sports, he had an even greater passion: music.

If music was his passion, Trevor was born at the right time. Growing up on the streets of Brooklyn, he had seen hip-hop culture developing all around him. In fact, other to-be famous rappers, like Jay-Z and the Notorious B.I.G., were growing up and being inspired in Brooklyn at the same time. When Trevor moved to Uniondale, his interest in hip-hop culture continued, and he began listening to New York City rappers like the group Public Enemy and the duo Eric B. & Rakim.

Like many other young hip-hop fans, Trevor began writing his own rhymes when he was practically still just a kid. By the time he was thirteen, he was rapping. Soon after, he started thinking about the possibility of a career in music. He and his cousin, Cut Monitor Milo, joined up with two friends, Charlie Brown and Dinco D. Together they started a rap crew called Leaders of the New School (or LONS). When Trevor was in tenth grade, he dropped out of high school to pursue music full time.

Becoming Busta Rhymes

In almost no time at all, LONS got its first record deal. They signed with Elektra Records in 1989, when Trevor was just seventeen years old. Before the young foursome even knew what hit them, they were touring with their heroes, Public Enemy. Public Enemy was fresh from the release of their first two albums, *Yo! Bum Rush the Show* and *It Takes a Nation of Millions to Hold Us Back*. They were huge successes, making Public Enemy one of the biggest rap crews of the time—and one of the first to have mainstream success. Their music was **revolutionary**, and the group was making a name for itself with controversial, hard-hitting, political lyrics.

Trevor and all the members of LONS were huge fans of Public Enemy, and they were thrilled when the group began taking them under their wing. In fact, Public Enemy's lead rapper, Chuck D, gave Trevor the name that would stick with him the rest of his career. Trevor reminded Chuck of the NFL wide receiver George "Busta" Rhymes. So he started calling Trevor Busta Rhymes. The name stuck fast, and it's been Trevor's stage name ever since.

Unfortunately, not everything about the relationship with Public Enemy was wonderful. Busta and the other crewmembers were just teenagers, straight from high school. But the members of Public Enemy didn't have mercy on them. They were determined to show them what it took to make it in the

How did Trevor Smith Jr. become Busta Rhymes? It was thanks to Public Enemy's lead singer, Chuck D. The young musician reminded Chuck of a pro football player called Busta Rhymes.

music industry. In an interview with Prairie Miller for nyrock.com, Busta recalled what it was like to have the members of Public Enemy as **mentors** during this early stage of their career:

> "It was kind of discouraging at some points. The way they would do things, it would feel almost as if they didn't want us to be around. Like we were getting on their nerves. And it was pretty much just a test of the faith and the dedication, and the commitment and the dire sacrifice that they wanted to see whether or not we were willing to make, to even be worthy of being a part of their affiliation. And I respected it a lot later on. But at the time, I thought they were . . . [jerks]."

The First Album

In the end, however, touring and working with Public Enemy provided many valuable lessons. Busta and his crew, however frustrated they may have become, stuck with it, and their commitment paid off. In 1991, LONS released its first studio album, *A Future Without a Past.* . . . Hip-hop still wasn't that big in the mainstream, but the album was an instant success on urban radio.

Like much of what is now called "old-school" hip-hop, most of the album's songs had lighthearted lyrics. The dominant themes were partying and boasting about their skills as MCs. But a few of the songs leaned toward "conscious hip-hop," which talks about social and political issues. The song "Teachers, Don't Teach Us Nonsense!!" was the last cut on the album, and it charged that the subjects taught in public school were irrelevant to the lives of black, inner-city youth. It insightfully claimed that young people who were acting out and labeled "problem" kids were just reacting to their environment, including an educational system that was not addressing their needs.

With their popularity on the rise, LONS began shaping their image and views. The group became more socially and politically minded, and they started associating with the Native Tongues Posse. The Native Tongues was a loose collective of hip-hop groups in the New York area in the eighties and early nineties. The groups and artists who were part of the Native Tongues had a huge influence on the development of East Coast hip-hop music, encouraging political or "conscious" hip-hop that had positive messages aimed at the black community. The Posse had close ties to DJ Afrika Bambaataa's Universal Zulu Nation and also believed in uplifting black youths through hip-hop culture.

The East Coast Scene

The core members of the Native Tongues Posse were Jungle Brothers, De La Soul, and A Tribe Called Quest. Over time, other artists like Queen Latifah, the Black Sheep, and LONS became associated with the crew. What was happening on the East Coast, however, with the Native Tongues Posse was in direct contrast with what was happening on the West Coast with gangsta rap.

Hip-hop started in New York City, and when it finally made it to radio, East Coast artists were the first to dominate the airwaves. But in the late 1980s, that began to change. West Coast artists quickly gained fans and challenged the East's dominance. From day one, hip-hop music was controversial. But the old-school style and political and socially conscious themes would soon look innocent and naïve compared with what the West Coast was about to produce.

In the late eighties, some East Coast hip-hop was already considered "hardcore." The Philadelphia MC, Schoolly D is believed to be the first MC to use the word "gangster" in his music, and he was a pioneer of the hardcore style on the East

Coast. A Bronx crew called Boogie Down Productions took the new hardcore style even further with the album *Criminal Minded*. The album's cover art showed the rappers brandishing guns, another first in hip-hop, and the song's themes included drugs, prostitution, and a first-person crime narrative. But even these controversial moves were about to look tame compared to what was next.

Los Angeles of the 1980s and 1990s was often the scene of gang activity. Some rappers were drawn into the gang culture, while others only rapped about it. The violence experienced on the street led to a new form of rap—gangsta rap.

Going Gangsta

As the Native Tongues Posse was focusing on uplifting the black community through hip-hop, some new West Coast artists were blowing up in a big way. The new artists were mostly from South Central Los Angeles, where gang warfare raged. The Crips and the Bloods (the two largest gangs in the area) dominated the neighborhoods. Hip-hop music had always been music from the street, so it should have come as no

Yes, it is Detective Tutuola—Fin—from Law & Order: SVU. But before that, he was Ice-T, gangsta rapper. His song "6 in the Mornin'" is considered by many to be the first gangsta rap song.

surprise that hip-hop artists from the L.A. area would feature gangster themes in their music.

In 1987, Los Angeles rapper Ice-T released the single "6 in the Mornin'." Ice-T had been talking about guns and pimping, and calling people **derogatory** names in his songs for years, but "6 in the Mornin'" is widely considered the first official gangsta rap song. The next year, a rap crew called N.W.A. released their solo album, *Straight Outta Compton*. With songs like "Straight Outta Compton" and "Gangsta, Gangsta," they took the gangsta themes even further. In 1992, the DJ, producer, and sometimes-MC, Dr. Dre released an album called *The Chronic*. The music he produced had a more laid-back rhythm than previous hip-hop albums. Called G-funk, it quickly became the most popular musical style for West Coast and gangsta rap. By the mid-nineties, the West Coast artists would take over as the industry's leaders, leaving East Coast artists scrambling to reclaim their empire.

Gangsta rap's near total dominance, however, was still a few years away. Back on the East Coast, the Native Tongues Posse and other political and conscious hip-hop outfits were getting their message out. In 1993, LONS released its second album, *T.I.M.E. (The Inner Mind's Eye)*. The album showed the Native Tongues' influence. It was more socially aware and **Afrocentric**. The lyrics were deeper than those on LONS's debut album. They were less focused on boasts and partying and more concerned with issues facing the black community. Disappointingly for the crew, the album overall wasn't as successful as their solo effort, but the single "What's Next" grabbed the top spot on the *Billboard* Hot Rap Singles chart.

Once the music world learned about Busta Rhymes, there was no stopping him. He quickly rose to the top. Eventually, the music world wasn't big enough to hold Busta and all his talents.

3

Hitting the Charts and the Silver Screen

The year 1993 was big for Busta Rhymes on a personal level as well. That year, his first child, a son, was born. Busta was entering fatherhood at a young age; he was just twenty-one. But family had always been important in his life. Today, he sees being a father as more important than being a musician or actor. But while Busta's personal life was entering a whole new phase, a chapter in his professional life was about to come to an end.

LONS were establishing themselves as an important voice in the hip-hop world. Not everything, however, was well with the group. As soon as LONS began having success, people started to zero in on Busta Rhymes. He had a deep voice, rapid-fire delivery, and an energetic (to the point of seeming sometimes manic) stage presence that drew fans. His rapping also had a unique, Jamaican-influenced flow that set Busta apart from other rappers. Whenever LONS performed, it seemed Busta couldn't help but steal the show. Soon there were tensions in the group. A now-infamous confrontation occurred between the group members during an appearance on the television show *Yo! MTV Raps*. It was suddenly clear to the world that LONS was breaking up.

The MTV incident was embarrassing, but it was another television appearance that marked the end for LONS and the beginning for Busta Rhymes. LONS had collaborated with A Tribe Called Quest on a popular single called "Scenario." The rap crews were invited to the *Arsenio Hall Show* to perform the single. Once again, Busta stole the show. When Elektra Records saw Busta's live performance on the popular entertainment program, they offered Busta his own record contract. After that, LONS called it quits, and Busta went solo.

Into the Limelight

It might have been all over for LONS, but things were just beginning for Busta. Suddenly, new opportunities were around every corner. Some of those opportunities came in the form of acting roles. Ever since rappers started making it big in the music world, they were showing up in Hollywood as well. The movie *Wild Style* had come out in 1982. It was about hip-hop music, break dancing, and graffiti, and it was the first movie about hip-hop culture.

Soon rappers were all over the silver screen. However, they weren't just appearing in movies specifically about hip-hop culture. It seemed that moviemakers felt having a rapper in the cast could give a film street **credibility** and attract the urban market. At first rappers only made cameo appearances. If they did get speaking roles, they played rappers, gangsters, or other typecast parts. But some hip-hop artists showed remarkable versatility, coming through with real acting skills. Within a few years, rappers were appearing in action movies, dramas, and comedies, and playing all different types of roles. It's a trend that has only gotten bigger over time. Today,

HITTING THE CHARTS AND THE SILVER SCREEN

rappers and former rappers like Will Smith, Ice-T, Ice Cube, Queen Latifah, LL Cool J, Snoop Dogg, Mos Def, DMX, and Ludacris have all launched successful acting careers. Some of them have even made it bigger as actors than they have as rappers.

In 1993, Busta made his film debut as Jawaan in the comedy *Who's the Man?* Set in Harlem, another section of New York City, the film told the story of two barbers who try to solve a murder (to much misadventure and mayhem). Busta was one of more than fifty rappers who made cameo appearances in the film. The short jaunt on the silver screen gave him a taste for acting. His next movie role came in famed director John Singleton's 1995 film, *Higher Learning*, a drama that starred fellow rapper Ice Cube. The movie was about a group of college freshmen at the fictitious Columbus University. In their first year of college, they struggle with issues like racism, rape, sexuality, and individuality. Busta Rhymes played a small supporting role in the film.

Going Solo

In 1996, Busta Rhymes released his debut solo album, *The Coming*. The single "Woo Hah!! Got You All in Check" hit the top 10 on the *Billboard* Hot 100 chart and earned a Grammy Award nomination for Best Rap Solo Performance. The album made its way to the #6 spot on the *Billboard* 200 album chart and was eventually certified **platinum**. The title, *The Coming*, was a reference to the apocalypse, the end of the world that is predicted in the Bible. It was an end-times theme that Busta would carry through many of his albums.

Despite the end-times title and hardcore lyrics, *The Coming* was filled with light songs. While the West Coast was getting huge with gangsta, Busta Rhymes was making a name for himself with a more old-school style and songs mostly boasting about his skills as an MC. The album also showed Busta's commitment to hip-hop as feel-good party music, a commitment that fewer hip-hop artists of his generation shared.

But Busta's split from LONS, and his by-now successful solo recording and movie career, didn't mean he was above **collaborating** with other artists. In fact, he began working with a group of up-and-coming hip-hop artists, and together they started a new crew called Flipmode Squad. Rah Digga, Rampage, Lord Have Mercy, Spliff Star, and Baby Sham were some of the artists in the squad. Many of the Flipmode members would appear on Busta's future albums.

Hit Making

Busta Rhyme's second solo album, *When Disaster Strikes*, was released in 1997. The "Intro" single warns there are only two and a half years left before the new millennium brings disaster and destruction. It then claims the disaster and destruction will come in the form of the Flipmode Squad, who will lay everyone out with their devastating, mind-blowing rhymes. Once again, despite the doomsday theme, the album is all party and **bravado**. The singles "Things We Be Doin' for Money (Part One)" and "Things We Be Doin' for Money (Part Two)" focused much more on violent themes, but overall the album's lyrics are mostly dedicated to Busta's skills as an MC. The theme was becoming classic Busta Rhymes.

When Disaster Strikes quickly became the top hip-hop album in the country. It was successful on the popular-music scene as well, with the single "Put Your Hands Where My Eyes Could See" shooting sky high. The album hit #3 on the *Billboard* 200 album chart. Busta Rhymes's career was moving along like a dream. At just twenty-four years old, he had already accomplished more than many professional musicians accomplish in a lifetime.

The apocalyptic themes continued with *E.L.E. (Extinction Level Event): The Final World Front*, which came out in 1998. This time, guns, violence, and other hardcore themes featured

HITTING THE CHARTS AND THE SILVER SCREEN

Collaborating is an important part of hip-hop music. Busta has collaborated with many other stars of the rap world. Rah Digga even became part of Busta's crew, Flipmode Squad. She has also appeared on several of Busta's albums.

more prominently in Busta's lyrics. Gangsta rap was now the most popular hip-hop music in the world, and it seemed Busta was changing with the times. He still was not a gangsta rapper, but he had definitely left the old school music and lyrics behind for a darker, edgier, grimier style. But the party was still on with the sexually explicit single "What's It Gonna Be?!" with Janet Jackson. The single scored another top-10 rating. It became the top rap single in the country and hit #3 on the *Billboard* Hot 100 chart.

She comes from a very famous family, but Janet Jackson has become a highly regarded artist in her own right. Janet and Busta had a #3 hit with their single "What's It Gonna Be?!"

HITTING THE CHARTS AND THE SILVER SCREEN

Fans liked the changes in Busta's style shown in *E.L.E.*, and it was considered his best album to date. Years later, after the September 11, 2001, attack on the World Trade Center, some people would also look back and see the album as eerily **prophetic**. Its cover art features New York City's skyline, including the World Trade Center, ablaze from a catastrophic event.

In 1998, Busta had other successes as well. He made his first appearance (or rather his voice did) in a children's film when he played the voice of the Reptar Wagon in *The Rugrats Movie*. He also released a collaborative album with the Flipmode Squad called *The Imperial Album*. The album was released under their Flipmode Records label. The late 1990s had been very good for Busta, and he could only imagine what a new century would bring.

The new millennium brought new opportunities for Busta Rhymes, and not all of them involved music. But he wasn't about to give up his hip-hop career. In 2002, Busta performed with Pharrell Williams at the Summer Stage Concert Series in New York's Central Park.

4
The New Millennium

The year 2000 was big for Busta movie-wise. He had two films come out and pushed his acting to a new level. He played Rasaan in John Singleton's *Shaft* (a remake of the 1971 movie), the story of a detective trying to solve a racially motivated murder. In the movie, Busta starred alongside famous actors Samuel L. Jackson, Toni Collette, Vanessa Williams, Jeffrey Wright, Mekhi Phifer, and Christian Bale.

That year Busta also had an important role in the movie *Finding Forrester*. Busta felt that *Finding Forrester* was his biggest accomplishment in his acting career to that date. It's the story of Jamal Wallace, a black teenager from the inner city who is accepted into a prestigious prep school. He has a difficult time adjusting to his new life and encounters prejudice at the school, but he also befriends a reclusive author, William Forrester, played by screen legend Sean Connery. Busta played the role of Terrell

Wallace, Jamal's older brother. In an interview with Prairie Miller for nyrock.com, Busta talked about his role in *Finding Forrester* as an important step in his acting career:

> "I think this is probably the first film that I can honestly say makes a conscious effort to separate Busta Rhymes the rapper from Busta Rhymes the actor. Most of the times I would get film opportunities where I'm Busta Rhymes the rapper as a character in a film. . . . But as an actor, I want to establish something new and fresh, that people can appreciate and love just as much, if not more so. And I just try to make sure that I build something there that can also secure the food on the table, if and when I decide to not be Busta Rhymes the rapper no more."

The comment was a little hint that, although Busta Rhymes clearly loves his music career and place in the hip-hop industry, he doesn't expect it to last forever. There may come a time when fans no longer buy his albums. Or there may come a time when he just doesn't want to be in the studio spitting rhymes anymore. When either of those things happens, then Busta knows it will be time to walk away. There would be points in the next few years when it seemed that perhaps that day was near.

Not Afraid of Controversy

In 2000, Busta released his fourth solo studio album, *Anarchy*. The album showed Busta's growing commitment to hardcore themes. It seemed every album Busta released was harder, tougher, more explicit, more violent, and more controversial than the last. For example, "Salute Da Gods!!," the first song on *Anarchy*, contained shocking (and some people would say disrespectful and tasteless) lyrics about the infamous school shooting in Columbine, Colorado.

THE NEW MILLENNIUM

The shooting was a tragic incident in which two teens opened fire on their schoolmates, killing twelve students and one teacher, and wounding more than twenty other people. Soon after, violence in movies, music, and video games came under fire as possible contributors to the conditions that caused the tragedy. Busta's lyrics, however, didn't seem to take that charge too seriously.

Even with his controversial lyrics, however, Busta Rhymes still remained one of the more party-oriented artists in the

The Columbine High School shooting found its way into Busta's music in 2000. Some people called the song "Salute Da Gods!!" disrespectful, shocking, and tasteless in its references to the tragedy.

hip-hop world. The *Anarchy* album went platinum quickly. It also marked the turn of the century and ended the era of Busta's apocalyptic themes. It was the end of another era as well. After the album, Busta left Elektra Records, the label that had now carried him for over ten years, and signed with J Records.

New Label, New Artist

In an article by Alan Sculley for citybeat.com, Busta talked about the career move. He said that he was growing as a person and an artist. He was quoted as saying he felt like it was time for a change, and J Records felt right:

> "It was just time to move on.... You know, [J Records] was new and fresh and it felt like [Clive Davis, the owner] had a new approach on doing things as far as business was concerned, and I just wanted to experience it. It was looking good, it was feeling good. It was relevant to the grand scheme of what I was trying to do."

He continued to pursue that grand scheme with yet another solo album. Despite the doomsday warnings of his previous four albums, the world did not end with the turn of the century. The new millennium had arrived, the world was still intact, and Busta was recording again. He changed his focus from one of apocalyptic death and destruction to one of rebirth. In 2001, he released his fifth solo album. In keeping with the theme of rebirth, he titled the album *Genesis*, after the first book of the Bible. The book of Genesis is the Judeo-Christian story of creation, and with a new record deal and new attitude toward his career, Busta felt it was an appropriate title for his new album.

That same year, Busta also released a greatest hits album called *Total Devastation: The Best of Busta Rhymes*. In 2002, his sixth solo album, *It Ain't Safe No More*, hit store shelves. It generated one hit, "I Know What You Want," featuring the Flipmode Squad and Mariah Carey, but other than that, the response to the album was only so-so. A second greatest hits album, *Turn It Up: The Very Best of Busta Rhymes*, followed up the release. It seemed like Busta was putting out albums left and right, but that wasn't necessarily a sign of things going well in his career.

Signing with J Records had seemed like the right move, but Busta's fans weren't responding to his new albums the way he had hoped. Sales were lower than ever before, and it seemed that perhaps the fans just weren't feeling him anymore. Busta had now been in the game for more than ten years, and his albums were no longer distinguishing themselves in sales or on the charts. In an interview for nyrock.com, Busta revealed that sometimes he felt frustrated with music and torn between pursuing new interests and giving the fans what they'd come to expect:

> "[In] rapping, you have to kinda carefully and gradually take people into the new places that you want to go. Because most of the time the audience is just so stubborn with wanting to get what they always loved you for, that when you start to change on 'em, they feel like you ain't being loyal to what you was to them. Or what they were to you. . . . When you're making music, you gotta constantly feed them what they want to eat, and gradually give them taste tests on the stuff that you want to introduce them to feeding on. And hope that they embrace it."

Unfortunately, fans weren't biting on what Busta was now feeding them, and he was faced with a dilemma: try to go back to what had worked in the past or do something completely new. Going backward didn't seem like a good idea. Fans had

One of the biggest names in hip-hop is Dr. Dre. He's a musician, a producer, and a businessman. Dr. Dre has also helped many young rappers on their way to success. One of those was Busta Rhymes.

heard it all before, and Busta wanted to move forward and grow, not the other way around. Plus, too many artists in the musical world fall flat by trying to recapture the glory of their past, unable to realize that it won't be original the second time around, and therefore won't have the same magic it once had.

    The answer seemed clear. If Busta wanted to stay hot in the hip-hop world, he needed to reinvent himself. He planned to do just that. Busta left J Records, and in 2004, he signed with Aftermath Entertainment, Dr. Dre's label. He released *The Artist Collection*, a compilation album of some of his previous work. Then he went into the studio with Dre, and fans heard . . . nothing.

It was a new version of Busta Rhymes that emerged in 2005. Gone were the dreadlocks that he had worn for years. Besides a new look, he had a new label. More important, one year later, he had his first album to debut at #1!

Number One for the First Time

Nothing was coming from the studio. Fans weren't sure what was happening with Busta Rhymes. For more than a decade he'd been pumping out the albums. For over ten years he'd churned out music like there was no tomorrow, which many of his albums claimed there wasn't. Now months passed with no sign of a new album. What had happened? Was Busta throwing in the hip-hop towel? Was he relinquishing his crown to a new generation?

Then there was a sign. Something big was definitely happening with Busta Rhymes. Fans knew because, in 2005, he did something almost unthinkable. He cut off his trademark dreadlocks—the dreadlocks he'd been growing since he signed his very first record deal when he was seventeen years old. It was all caught on film, and Busta Rhymes said it was symbolic of a new beginning for him as a musician. He states on his Web site that he began changing the minute he signed with Aftermath, and that he is now a whole new man:

> "I'm a new dude now, that's all people need to know. Everything about me is new. New deal, new money, new look, new sound and a new staff to promote my [music]. It's a complete restructure. And it all started with switching my record company."

Although Busta saw the haircut as a major symbolic event in his life, he also apparently had a sense of humor about what, for many people, would have been a traumatic ordeal. The BBC quoted him saying that, at long last, he had finally earned his father's respect. All it took was cutting his hair:

> "It didn't matter how much respect I gained as a man with dreads, my father couldn't deal with it. When I cut my hair that was the happiest day of his life!"

A Long Time Comin'

Busta Rhymes spent almost three years in the studio working with Dr. Dre on the new album. It was a completely different experience from anything else he'd ever had in music making. Busta admits that he's typically a rush-ahead, bang-em-out artist. Dre, in contrast, believes in taking it slow. Like the laid-back rhythms in his G-funk album, *The Chronic*, Dre knows that some good things only come when they're given a little extra time. On his Web site, Busta said that he learned a lot from Dre's easy-does-it approach:

> "Patience has definitely been my best weapon on this project, because Dre will never rush anything. He's the most patient [person] I've ever met, and I've learned that important lesson from him. It's been a

NUMBER ONE FOR THE FIRST TIME

deep experience overall because it's really been just me and him in the studio most of the time. We both knew that I needed to challenge myself to put together something that went beyond anything I've ever done before."

The Big Bang featured some of the biggest names in music history. Rick James, the late reggae legend, performed on the album. So did Stevie Wonder, another artist with a decades-long career.

The new album would definitely go beyond anything Busta had done before. By late 2005, the buzz was growing on the streets as fans anticipated the release. By early 2006, that buzz was becoming a roar. Some of Busta's new songs had been leaked to the Internet, and they got everybody talking. There were rumors, too, that the album would feature some of the greatest artists in the business as guests. By the time the album was released on June 13, 2006, fans were practically lined up salivating at record-store doors.

The album was called *The Big Bang*, and true to its name, it exploded onto the music scene. For the first time in his fifteen-year career, Busta Rhymes had an album debut at #1 on the *Billboard* 200 album chart. The album featured songs with legends like Stevie Wonder and the late Rick James. For Busta, working with these men was an incredible honor. It also showed just how far Busta Rhymes had come as an artist, and confirmed that he too was now one of the legends of the music world.

Tragedy

More than ten years after his first solo album was released, Busta Rhymes was finally on top of the charts. Many people consider the album his very best work, the crowning achievement of his career. Busta Rhymes was on top of the world, or at least, he should have been. But instead the best moment of Busta's career was hugely dampened by tragedy.

On February 5, 2006, just over four months before *The Big Bang*'s release, Busta's longtime bodyguard, Israel Ramirez, was shot and killed. It happened outside of a recording studio where Busta was shooting a video for one of the singles. Apparently, an argument broke out, got heated, and then erupted into gunfire. What exactly went down, however, is still unclear, and Ramirez's death remains unsolved, and his killer unknown.

The tragedy had a huge impact on Busta, who in an interview for *XXL* magazine said he just couldn't understand why someone would target his friend:

> "[Israel] displayed a level of love to his friends that was unlike anything that I've seen. . . . Who in the world would think that such a demon energy could come amongst that love energy and take the life of a man that in no shape, form, or fashion, not in the slightest way contributed to any of what was brought on? I could never answer that question. Every day since that day I been going through this thing that's been really confusing . . . me—because it just doesn't add up."

The incident, however, wasn't just a personal loss for Busta. It also became a bit of a scandal when Busta, who police believe may have witnessed the shooting or something relevant to the shooting, refused to cooperate with the investigation. Although the police repeatedly asked him to give them any information he might have, Busta refused to talk, and that got a lot of people upset.

Legal Woes

Soon after the shooting, other incidents began to affect Busta's reputation as well. Throughout his career, Busta has been known as a rapper who stays on the right side of the law. In an industry whose image is regularly tarnished by rappers being arrested for everything from traffic violations to murder charges, Busta was considered a breath of fresh air and a reliable law abider. That image began to change in 2006. Refusing to cooperate with the police in the investigation into the shooting that killed his bodyguard brought Busta a lot of bad press. That bad press continued the next month when stories claiming Busta had lashed out at a gay fan and made **homophobic** comments flew around the news. In March, a fan also accused Busta of assault. Then, in August, he was arrested for allegedly assaulting a man in a parking lot.

That was the first of what would be a string of arrests. He was arrested four times in less than a year. The next arrest came in December 2006. Once again it was for assault, this time of Busta's driver. A few months later, in February 2007, Busta was stopped for a traffic violation and then arrested for driving with a suspended license. Just a few months after that, in May 2007, he was arrested again, this time for suspicion of driving under the influence of alcohol. In court, Busta twice rejected plea bargains, and was scheduled for four separate trials.

Fighting for the Top

It was a roller-coaster year for Busta, but he was determined to keep his new place on top. In his interview with Melanie Cornish for nobodysmiling.com, he talked about how he deals with the negative things, and how he presents them to his kids. He also responded to the criticism that hip-hop sends the wrong messages to kids, and that rappers are bad role models. Like many rappers, he says that the music they make is about real life, and you can't be afraid of the truth:

> "I conceal nothing from my kids as I don't want them to know a fairy tale side of life. You know we talk about painting good pictures and making nice examples for kids but they also have to see the negative [stuff] that comes with how we are being the type of people we are, black people and they have to know how to deal with it, so they have to know what is going on on the good side as well as the bad. They can see how I am handling it and its like when they grown up and

NUMBER ONE FOR THE FIRST TIME

they have [stuff] to handle on a negative level, there is a certain blueprint on how they have to handle things and you know be instinctive and trust their judgment. You know they will know how to handle things both good and bad."

Busta Rhymes was trying not to focus on the bad. After all, he'd just had the biggest album of his career, and he was hard at work on his next one, *Before Hell Freezes Over*. Busta is also making his way back to the big screen in his first movie since 2004's *Full Clip*. In his newest theatrical venture, Busta starred as Al Bowen, a murderous gangster and drug dealer, in the movie *Order of Redemption*.

It appears that, after everything he's done and everything he's been through, Busta Rhymes is now counting his blessings. On his Web site he states that, at the end of the day, he's just grateful that he's always had hip-hop music:

"[We've been blessed] just having hip-hop as a vehicle to channel everything through. I mean, what would we be doing if hip-hop wasn't here? A lot of successful people in the game need to think about that and appreciate it. Me and Dre definitely do."

What would Busta do if he didn't have hip-hop? It's a question fans hope he'll never have to answer. After all, they want Busta to keep going, keep turning out the records, and banging out the hits. And, if he has anything to say about it, this legend is going to keep giving them what they want and making rap music for years to come.

CHRONOLOGY

1970s   Hip-hop is born in the Bronx section of New York City.

May 20, 1972   Trevor Tahiem Smith Jr.—Busta Rhymes—is born in Brooklyn, New York.

1980s   Hip-hop enters the music mainstream.

late 1980s   West Coast hip-hop challenges East Coast domination.

1987   Ice-T releases the first gangsta hit song.

1989   LONS signs with Elektra Records.

1991   LONS releases its first studio album.

1993   Busta becomes a father for the first time.

1993   Busta makes his film debut in *Who's the Man?*

1995   Busta costars in *Higher Learning*.

1996   Busta releases his first solo album.

1997   *When Disaster Strikes* is released.

1998   Busta's doomsday theme continues when *E.L.E. (Extinction Level Event): The Final World Front* is released.

1998   Busta voices the character of The Reptar Wagon in the children's film *The Rugrats Movie*.

2000   Busta costars in *Shaft* and *Finding Forrester*.

CHRONOLOGY

2000 Busta releases *Anarchy*.

2001 *Genesis* is released.

2004 Busta signs with Dr. Dre's label, Aftermath Entertainment.

Feb. 5, 2006 Busta's bodyguard, Israel Ramirez, is murdered, and Busta does not cooperate with the police in the investigation.

June 13, 2006 *The Big Bang* is released and debuts at #1.

August 2006 Busta is arrested for assault.

Dec. 2006 Busta is arrested again for assault.

Feb. 2007 Busta is charged with moving violations.

May 2007 Busta is arrested for suspected driving while intoxicated.

late 2007 *Before Hell Freezes Over* is released.

Accomplishments and Awards

Albums

1996   *The Coming*

1997   *When Disaster Strikes*

1998   *E.L.E. (Extinction Level Event): The Final World Front*

2000   *Anarchy*

2001   *Genesis*

            Total Devastation: The Best of Busta Rhymes

2002   *It Ain't Safe No More*

            Turn It Up: The Very Best of Busta Rhymes

2004   *The Artist Collection*

2006   *The Big Bang*

2007   *Before Hell Freezes Over*

Number-One Singles

1996   "Woo Hah!! Got You All in Check"

1997   "Dangerous"

1998   "Turn It Up/Fire It Up"

1999   "What's It Gonna Be?!" (with Janet Jackson)

2006   "Touch It"

DVDs

2002   *Slip 'N' Slide: All Star Weekend*

2003   *I Know What You Want*

2004   *Everything Remains Raw*

2007   *Busta Rhymes, DMX, and Mystikal on DVD*

2007   *Smack, Vol. 12: Ludacris and Busta Rhymes*

Films

1993   *Who's the Man?*

1995   *Higher Learning*

1998   *The Rugrats Movie*

2000   *Finding Forrester*

             Shaft

2002   *Narc*

             Halloween: Resurrection

2003   *Death of a Dynasty*

2004   *Full Clip*

Awards and Recognitions

1999 Source Hip-Hop Music Award: Music Video of the Year ("What's It Gonna Be?!" with Janet Jackson).

2000 Soul Train Music Award: R&B/Soul or Rap Music Video ("What's It Gonna Be?!" with Janet Jackson).

Books

Bogdanov, Vladimir, Chris Woodstra, Steven Thomas Erlewine, and John Bush (eds.). *All Music Guide to Hip-Hop: The Definitive Guide to Rap and Hip-Hop.* San Francisco, Calif.: Backbeat Books, 2003.

Chang, Jeff. *Can't Stop Won't Stop: A History of the Hip-Hop Generation.* New York: Picador, 2005.

Emcee Escher and Alex Rappaport. *The Rapper's Handbook: A Guide to Freestyling, Writing Rhymes, and Battling.* New York: Flocabulary Press, 2006.

George, Nelson. *Hip Hop America.* New York: Penguin, 2005.

Kusek, Dave, and Gerd Leonhard. *The Future of Music: Manifesto for the Digital Music Revolution.* Boston, Mass.: Berkley Press, 2005.

Light, Alan (ed.). *The Vibe History of Hip Hop.* New York: Three Rivers Press, 1999.

Walker, Ida. *Hip-Hop Around the World.* Broomall, Pa.: Mason Crest, 2008.

Waters, Rosa. *Hip-Hop: A Short History.* Broomall, Pa.: Mason Crest, 2007.

Watkins, S. Craig. *Hip Hop Matters: Politics, Pop Culture, and the Struggle for the Soul of a Movement.* Boston, Mass.: Beacon Press, 2006.

Web Sites

Busta Rhymes
www.bustarhymes.com

Busta Rhymes on MTV
www.mtv.com/music/artist/rhymes_busta/artist.jhtml

Busta Rhymes on MySpace
www.myspace.com/bustarhymes

Busta Rhymes on VH1
www.vh1.com/artists/az/rhymes_busta/artist.jhtml

Glossary

Afrocentric—Centered on Africa or people from Africa.

bravado—A real or pretend display of courage or boldness.

collaborating—Working with someone else to produce something.

compilation—Something created by bringing together things from various places.

controversial—Causing strong disagreement or disapproval.

credibility—Believability.

culture—The beliefs, customs, practices, and social behavior of a particular nation or people.

derogatory—Expressing a low opinion or negative criticism about someone or something.

funk—A music style that is based on jazz, the blues, and soul, and is characterized by a heavy bass and backbeat.

homophobic—Having an irrational hatred, disapproval, or fear of homosexuality or homosexuals.

mainstream—The ideas, actions, and values that are most widely accepted by a group or society.

mentors—People who are more experienced at something who act as advisers and supporters to less experienced individuals.

GLOSSARY

platinum—A designation that a recording has sold a million units.

prophetic—Predicting something that eventually occurs.

revolutionary—So new and different that it causes a major change in something.

samples—Bits of previously recorded music that is used in another recording.

Index

A Future Without a Past... (album) 25
Aftermath Entertainment 45
Anarchy (album) 40, 42
Artist Collection, The (album) 45

Before Hell Freezes Over (album) 53
Big Bang, The (album) 49, 50
Busta Rhymes
    and Aftermath Entertainment 45
    and early solo career 32–37
    and films 33–40, 53
    and J Records 42–45
    and legal issues 51–52
    and LONS 23–32
    and youth 21–23

Chuck D 23, 24
Coming, The (album) 33

Dr. Dre 29, 44, 48

E.L.E. (Extinction Level Event):The Final World Front (album) 34, 37
Elektra Records 23, 32, 42

Finding Forrester (film) 39, 40
Flipmode Squad 34, 35, 37, 43
Full Clip (film) 53

Genesis (album) 42

Higher Learning (film) 33

Imperial Album, The (album) 37
It Ain't Safe No More (album) 43

Jackson, Janet 36

Leaders of the New School (LONS) 23, 25, 26, 29, 31, 32, 34

Order of Redemption (film) 53

Ramirez, Israel 50, 51
Rugrats Movie, The (film) 37

Shaft (film) 39
Smith Jr., Trevor Tahiem (see Busta Rhymes)

T.I.M.E. (The Inner Mind's Eye) (album) 29
Total Devastation: The Best of Busta Rhymes (album) 42
Turn It Up: The Very Best of Busta Rhymes (album) 43

When Disaster Strikes (album) 34
Who's the Man? (film) 33

About the Author

Toby G. Hamilton was born in 1979 in Binghamton, NY. As an author and illustrator, Toby is interested in art's power as a tool of self-expression, social commentary, and political activism. Toby is especially interested in hip-hop's role in twenty-first century America and its increasing power as a revolutionary force around the world.

Picture Credits

Alan, Scott / PR Photos: front cover, p. 2
Bielawski, Adam / PR Photos: p. 24
Hatcher, Chris / PR Photos: p. 49
iStockphoto:
    Burkard, Sascha: p. 11
    Gearhart, Rosemarie: p. 27
    Lee, Renee: p. 41
    Schneider, Doug: p. 12
    Yakovlev, Alexander: p. 18
Kirkland, Dean / PR Photos: p. 8
Mayer, Janet / PR Photos: pp. 28, 36
PR Photos: pp. 30, 46
Thompson, Terry / PR Photos: pp. 35, 42
Wild1 / PR Photos: p. 38

To the best knowledge of the publisher, all other images are in the public domain. If any image has been inadvertently uncredited, please notify Harding House Publishing Service, Vestal, New York 13850, so that rectification can be made for future printings.